Kitten's Adventure

For Commander John Mervyn Jones R.N.V.R.(ret.)
for all his help and love

Also by Michele Coxon in Happy Cat Paperbacks
The Cat Who Lost His Purr
Where's My Kitten? A Hide-and-Seek Flap Book
Who Will Play With Me?

Kitten's Adventure

Michele Coxon

Happy Cat Books

Where is the sky?

Here, there and everywhere.

Where are the birds?

Here.

Where are the hens?

There.

Where are the pigs?

Everywhere.

Where are the ponies?

Here.

Where are the mice?

There.

Where are the cows?

Everywhere.

Where are the insects?

Here.

Where are the dogs?

There.

Where is daddy?

Here he is.

Where are my brother and sister?

There they are.

Where is mummy?

Here and nowhere else!

Goodnight. Sleep tight!

Text and illustrations copyright © Michele Coxon, 1997

The moral right of the author/illustrator has been asserted

This edition first published 1997 by Happy Cat Books, Bradfield, Essex CO11 2UT

Reprinted 1998

A CIP catalogue record for this book is available from the British Library

ISBN 1 899248 06 4 Paperback

ISBN 1899248 01 3 Hardback

Printed in Hong Kong by Wing King Tong

Happy Cat Paperbacks by Michele Coxon
for you to enjoy

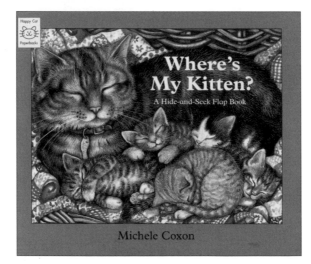